For Cynthia Fitzjohn and her class
S.H.

For David and Elizabeth
T.G.

ACKNOWLEDGEMENTS

Every effort has been made to trace the ownership of all copyrighted material and
to secure the necessary permissions to reprint these selections. In the event of any
questions arising as to the use of any material, the editor and the publisher,
while expressing regret for any inadvertent error, will be happy to make the
necessary correction in future printings.

Grateful acknowledgement is made to the following for
permission to reprint the copyrighted material listed below:

Galaxy Music Corporation for "Little Arabella Miller" from FINGERS AND THUMBS
by Anne Elliot. Copyright © 1933 Stainer & Bell Ltd. Used by permission
of Galaxy Music Corporation, New York, N.Y., sole U.S. agent.

Pitman Publishing, London, for "Mouse in a Hole"
from NUMBER RHYMES AND FINGER PLAYS
by Boyce and Bartlett, copyright © 1941. Reproduced by permission of
Pitman Publishing.

The publisher would like to acknowledge the authors of the following rhymes:
Mrs Wyn Daniel Evans for "Ten Galloping Horses,"
Emilie Poulson for "The Beehive" and Christina Rossetti for "The Pancake"

Library of Congress Cataloging in Publication Data
Clap your hands.
Summary: A collection of traditional rhymes with illustrations of the finger
actions that accompany them. 1. Finger play—Juvenile literature. 2. Nursery
rhymes—Juvenile literature. [1. Nursery rhymes. 2. Finger play] I. Hayes,
Sarah. II. Goffe, Toni, ill. GV1218.F5C52 1988   398′.8   87-16958
ISBN 0-688-07692-0   ISBN 0-688-07693-9 (lib. bdg.)

CLAP YOUR HANDS
FINGER RHYMES

Chosen by Sarah Hayes   *Illustrated by* Toni Goffe

CONTENTS

Lothrop, Lee & Shepard Books
New York

KNOCK AT THE DOOR

Knock at the door. Peep in. Lift the latch. And walk in.

Chin chopper, chin chopper, chin chopper, chin.

HERE IS THE CHURCH

Here is the church,

And here's the steeple.

Open the doors

I AM A COBBLER

I am a cobbler
And this is what I do:
Rap-tap-a-tap
To mend my shoe.

And see all the
people.

Here is the parson
Going upstairs,

And here he is
Saying his
prayers.

TWO FAT GENTLEMEN

 Two fat gentlemen met in a lane,

 Bowed most politely,

bowed once again.

How do you do,
How do you do,
And how do you do again?

 Two thin ladies met in a lane,
Bowed most politely, bowed once again.
How do you do,
How do you do,
And how do you do again?

Two tall policemen met in a lane,
Bowed most politely, bowed once again.
How do you do,
How do you do,
And how do you do again?

Two little schoolboys met in a lane,
Bowed most politely, bowed once again.
How do you do,
How do you do,
And how do you do again?

Two little babies met in a lane,
Bowed most politely, bowed once again.
How do you do,
How do you do,
And how do you do again?

9

TEN GALLOPING HORSES

Ten galloping horses came through the town.

Five were white and five were brown.

They galloped up

and galloped down;

Ten galloping horses came through the town.

11

THE
BEEHIVE

Here is the beehive,
Where are the bees?
Hidden away where
nobody sees.

Soon they come creeping
Out of the hive.

One and two and three, four, five.

LITTLE MOUSIE

Here's a little mousie
Peeking through a hole.

Peek to the left.

Peek to the right.

Pull your
head back in,

There's a
cat
in
sight!

MOUSE IN A HOLE

A mouse lived in
a little hole,

Lived softly in
a little hole,

When all was quiet
as quiet
can be...

OUT
POPPED
HE!

14

THREE LITTLE MONKEYS

Three little monkeys
Swinging from a tree,

Teasing Mr. Alligator,
"Can't catch me!"

Along came Mr. Alligator

Slowly as can be . . .

Then . . .

SNAP!

INCEY WINCEY SPIDER

Incey wincey spider
climbed up the water spout.

Down came the rain
and washed the spider out.

Out came the sun,
and dried up all the rain.

And incey wincey spider
climbed up the spout again.

CHOOK, CHOOK, CHOOK-CHOOK-CHOOK

Chook, chook, chook-chook-chook,
Good morning, Mrs. Hen.
How many chickens have you got?

Madam, I've got ten.

Four of them are yellow,

And four of them
are brown,

And two of them
are speckled red—

The nicest in the town!

GOOD THINGS TO EAT

| Will you have a cookie, | Or a piece of pie, | Or a striped candy stick? | Well, so will I. |

THREE LITTLE PUMPKINS

Three little pumpkins sitting on a wall,

A witch came riding by—

Ha-ha-ha! I'll take you all To make a pumpkin pie!

FIVE FAT PEAS

Five fat peas in a pea-pod pressed.

One grew, two grew, so did all the rest.

They grew and grew   and did not stop,   Until one day the pod went POP!

TEN FAT SAUSAGES

Ten fat sausages
sizzling in the pan,
Ten fat sausages
sizzling in the pan,

One went

POP

and another
went BANG.

There were eight fat sausages sizzling in the pan.

Eight fat sausages sizzling in the pan...

Six fat sausages sizzling in the pan...

Four fat sausages sizzling in the pan...

Two fat sausages sizzling in the pan,
Two fat sausages sizzling in the pan,
One went POP and another went BANG.
There were no fat sausages sizzling in the pan.

THE PANCAKE

Mix a pancake,
Stir a pancake,

Pop it in
the pan.

Fry the
pancake,

Toss the
pancake,

Catch it if you can.

PAT-A-CAKE

Pat-a-cake, pat-a-cake, baker's man,

Bake me a cake as fast as you can.

Pat it

and prick it,

and mark it with B,

And put it in the oven for Baby and me.

23

LITTLE TURTLE

There was a little turtle.

He lived in a box.

He swam in a puddle.

He climbed on the rocks.

He snapped at a mosquito.
He snapped at a flea.
He snapped at a minnow.
He snapped at me.

He caught the mosquito.
He caught the flea.
He caught the minnow.
But he didn't catch me.

ONE, TWO, THREE, FOUR, FIVE

One, two, three, four, five,

Once I caught a fish alive.

Six, seven, eight, nine, ten,

Then I let him go again.

Why did you let him go?
Because he bit my finger so.

Which finger did he bite?
This little finger on the right.

LITTLE ARABELLA MILLER

Little Arabella Miller
Found a woolly caterpillar.
First it crawled upon her mother,

Then upon her
baby brother.

All said,
"Arabella Miller,
Take away that
caterpillar!"

ROUND AND ROUND THE GARDEN

Round and round the garden, like a teddy bear;

One step,   two step,

Tickly under there!

IN A COTTAGE

In a cottage
in a wood

A little old man
at the window stood.

Saw a rabbit
running by

Knocking
at the
window.

"Help me!
Help me! Help!"
he said,

"Lest the
huntsman shoot
me dead."

"Come little rabbit,
Come to me,
Happy you shall be."

HOW MANY

How many people live at your house?

One, my mother,

Two, my father,

Three, my sister,

Four, my brother.

There's one more,
now let me see.

Oh yes, of course. It must be me!

DATE DUE

JUN. 29 1995		
JUL 05 '96		
■■■■■■		
■■ 1 3 ■■		
DEC 0 4 '96		
10-31-01		
MAR 0 2 2005		
GAYLORD		PRINTED IN U.S.A.